I'm not Ready!

Jonathan Allen

SCHOLASTIC INC.

Baby Owl was getting ready to go to preschool for the very first time. He and his mom were going to walk there with Small Squirrel and Mrs. Squirrel.

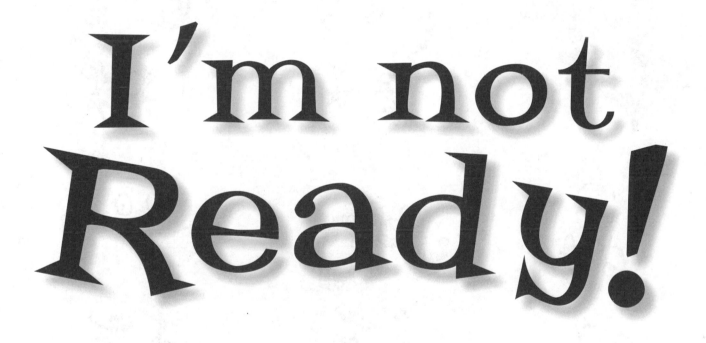

ISBN 978-0-545-64482-2

Text and illustrations copyright © 2011 by Jonathan Allen. All rights reserved. Published by Scholastic Inc., 557 Broadway, New York, NY 10012, by arrangement with Sterling Publishing Co., Inc. SCHOLASTIC and associated logos are trademarks and/or registered trademarks of Scholastic Inc.

12 11 10 9 8 7 6 5 4 3 2 1   13 14 15 16 17 18/0

Printed in the U.S.A.   40

First Scholastic printing, September 2013

The illustrations were prepared digitally by the author.
The text is set in Adobe Garamond Regular.

"Hurry up, Baby Owl," called Mom.
"Small Squirrel will be here soon."

"I'm not ready!" said Baby Owl.
"I'm putting my toys away."

"Putting your toys away?" said Mom.
"But you never put your toys away."

Small Squirrel and his mom arrived.
"Come on, Baby Owl," called Mom.
"Small Squirrel is here."

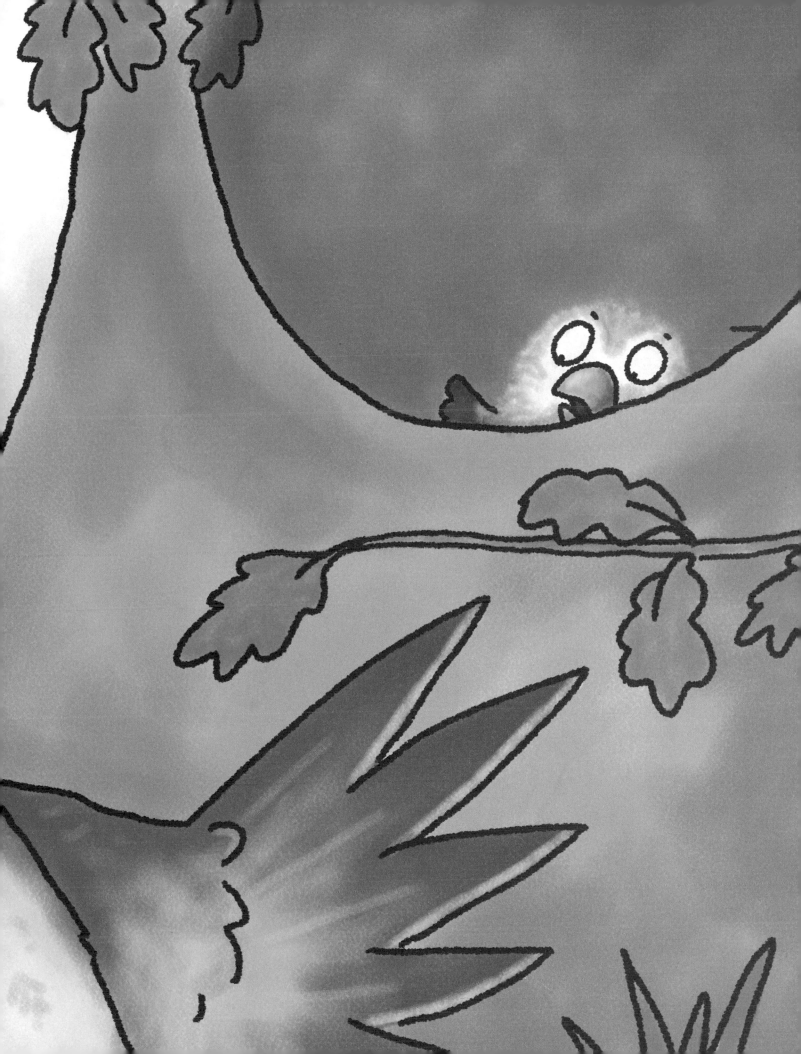

"I'm not ready!" said Baby Owl.
"I'm brushing my feathers!"

"It's hanging by the door!" said Mom.
"I can see it from here. Now hurry up!"

"But Owly's not ready!" said Baby Owl.
"His feathers need brushing too!"

"Baby Owl," said Mom, "you know
Owly doesn't have any feathers!
Now come down, we really have to go!"

"Brushing your feathers?" said Mom.
"But you never brush your feathers!
Please, Baby Owl, we have to go!"

"But I'm not ready!"
said Baby Owl.
"I can't find my backpack."

"I am NOT ready!"

cried Baby Owl. "It's not fair!
You're making me go to preschool
when I'm not ready!"

"Don't you want to go to preschool?"
asked Mom, giving him a hug.
"Come on, Baby Owl. It will be fun."

"All right, Mom," said Baby Owl.

When they got to preschool, Baby Owl cheered up. Little Rabbit, Baby Badger, and all his other friends were there.

"Put me down, Mom!" said Baby Owl. "I want to play with my friends!"

"All right," said Mom, "if you're sure that you're ready."

Baby Owl played happily all day.
He was still playing when Dad
came to pick him up.

"Come on, Baby Owl,"
said Dad. "It's time to go home!"

"But I'm not ready!" said Baby Owl.
"I'm playing with Small Squirrel."

"Small Squirrel's dad is here too," said
Dad. "We can walk home together."

That night, Mom asked, "Are you and Owly ready for a good night's sleep?" "We are," said Baby Owl. "I don't want to be late for preschool tomorrow."

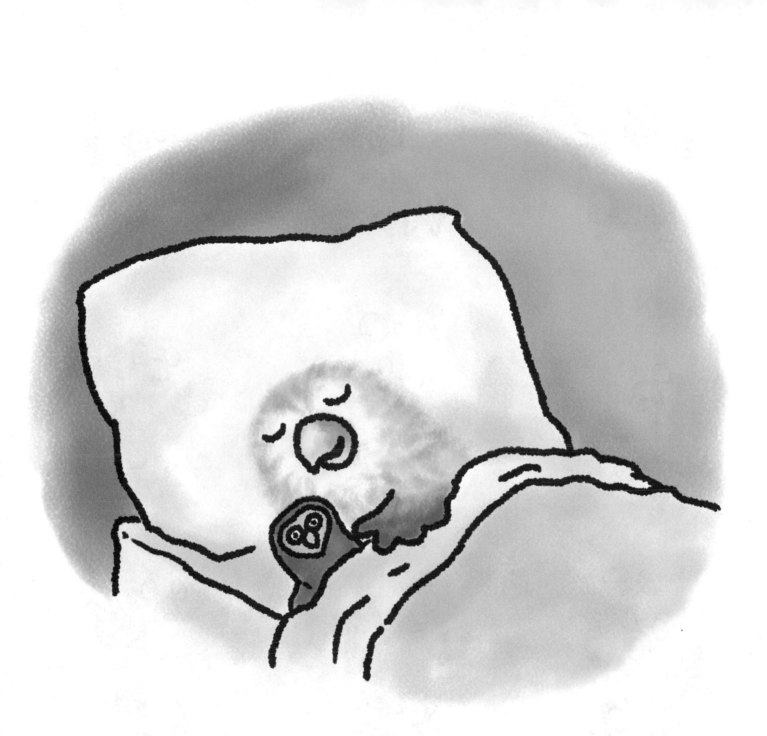

"Good night, Baby Owl," said Mom.
"Good night, Mom," said Baby Owl.